Changes
Changes
Changes

AN ANTHOLOGY
BY NEW WRITERS

NEW WRITERS' VOICES
READERS HOUSE
Literacy Volunteers of New York City

NEW WRITERS' VOICES™ was made possible by grants from: an anonymous foundation; Exxon Corporation; Scripps Howard Foundation; Philip Morris Companies, Inc.; Garry Trudeau and Penguin USA; and H. W. Wilson Foundation.

•   •

ATTENTION READERS: We would like to hear what you think about our books. Please send your comments or suggestions to:

    The Editors
    Literacy Volunteers of New York City
    121 Avenue of the Americas
    New York, NY 10013

•   •   •

99 98 97 96 95 94 93   10 9 8 7 6 5 4 3 2 1

First LVNYC Printing: April 1993

ISBN 1-56853-006-4

New Writers' Voices is a series of books published by Readers House, the publishing division of Literacy Volunteers of New York City Inc., 121 Avenue of the Americas, New York, NY 10013. The words, "New Writers' Voices," are a trademark of Readers House/Literacy Volunteers of New York City. READERS HOUSE and colophon are trademarks of Literacy Volunteers of New York City.

Cover designed by Paul Davis Studio; interior designed by Barbara Huntley.

The articles in this book were edited with the cooperation and consent of the authors. Every effort has been made to locate the copyright owners of material reproduced in this book. Omissions brought to our attention will be corrected in subsequent editions.

Executive Director, LVNYC: Lilliam Barrios-Paoli
Publishing Director, LVNYC: Nancy McCord
Managing Editor: ꟷꟷ Kirshner
Publishing Coordinator: Yvette Martinez-Gonzalez
Marketing/Production Manager: Elizabeth Bluemle
LVNYC is an affiliate of Literacy Volunteers of America.

ACKNOWLEDGMENTS

Literacy Volunteers of New York City gratefully acknowledges the generous support of the following foundations and corporations that made the publication of READERS HOUSE books possible: an anonymous foundation; Exxon Corporation; Scripps Howard Foundation; Philip Morris Companies, Inc.; Garry Trudeau and Penguin USA; and H. W. Wilson Foundation.

We deeply appreciate the contributions of the following suppliers: an anonymous donor (cover stock); Arcata Graphics Company (cover and text printing and binding) Boise Cascade Corporation (text stock); Cam Steel Rule Die Works Inc. (steel cutting die for display); ComCom Inc. (text typesetting); Delta Corrugated Container (corrugated display); MCUSA (display header); Phototype Color Graphics (cover color separations).

For their guidance, support and hard work, we are indebted to the LVNYC Board of Directors' Publishing Committee: James E. Galton, Marvel Comics Ltd.; Virginia Barber, Virginia Barber Literary Agency, Inc.; Doris Bass, Scholastic, Inc.; Jeff Brown; Jerry Butler; George P. Davidson, Ballantine Books; Joy M. Gannon, St. Martin's Press; Walter Kiechel, *Fortune*; Geraldine E. Rhoads; Virginia Rice, Reader's Digest; Martin Singerman, News America Publishing, Inc.; James L. Stanko, James Money Management, Inc.; and Arnold Schaab and F. Robert Stein of Pryor, Cashman, Sherman & Flynn.

Thanks also to George Davidson, Caron Harris, Steve Palmer, Katy Steinhilber and Tonya Wright of Ballantine Books for producing this book; Alison Mitchell for her thoughtful copyediting and suggestions; Stephanie Butler for research and to Candace Wainwright for proofreading.

We would also like to thank the tutors whose dedicated work with our student authors has enhanced our book. We would also like to thank the LVNYC center directors who helped the project progress. The following institutions and people also assisted with this project: KENTUCKY: Mary Pettey, Johnson County Literacy Project, Paintsville; NEW YORK: Patricia Medina and Carolyn Ferrell, Bronx Educational Services; Margaret Schrage, Flushing Adult Learning Center; Helen Morris and Janet Regina, LVA-Suffolk County, Bellport; Ann Wrafter, Eastern Parkway Learning Center, Brooklyn Public Library; OREGON: Virginia Tardaewether, Salem Even Start; PENNSYLVANIA: Barbara Gill, Reading Even Start; Mary J. Taylor, Lutheran Settlement House, Philadelphia; RHODE ISLAND: Ralph Fortune and Sally Gabb, Travelers Aid Society of Rhode Island, Providence; WASHINGTON: Sandra McNeil, Goodwill Adult Literacy Center, Seattle; Jon Nachman, Seattle Education Center, Metrocenter YMCA; WISCONSIN: Carol Gabler, LVA-Chippewa Valley, Eau Claire.

For their hard work and enthusiastic participation, we would like to thank our student authors.

Our thanks to Paul Davis Studio and Myrna Davis, Paul Davis, Lisa Mazur, Hajime Ando, Haruetai Muodtong and Chalkley Calderwood for their inspired design of the covers of these books. Thanks also to Barbara Huntley for her sensitive design of the interior of this book.

CONTENTS

Prayer

RAYMOND, Rhode Island

Please, God,
make us one family
and teach us
how to be united
to one another
and to be more kind
to one another.
And show us
how to care for one another.
And please show us
how to drag
the demons away.

Quiet Time

CARLA ELIJAH, New Jersey

I like the quiet time at night.
The quiet time is for me.
The night is the time for me.
The quiet time at night is for me.

I can do what I want to do.
No more children yelling, screaming
    or throwing toys.
No more children calling my name.
No one saying, "Mommy, I'm hungry.
    Fix me something to eat."
No more raising my voice.
The nighttime is for me.

I lay here in my bed,
Dreamin' what I want to do.
I dream I am a nurse.
I'm on top of the world,
Doin' what I want to do.
I'm goin' everywhere.
Don't have to worry about how I'm
    going to get there

'Cause I'm already there in my head.
I'm already all these things I want to be.
The nighttime is for me.

Don't have to worry.
Fixin' dinner's done
And the day is done.
The children are in bed,
Dreamin' about dreamland.
I can hear myself breathing.
I can hear myself singing.
The nighttime is for me.

I stand by my window,
Lookin' up above me.
I see the moon in the sky, the stars
    above me bright at night.
I look down below me
And I see a tree standing so still,
I see its shadow falling on a building.
No one is here but me.
The quiet time is for me.
The nighttime is just for me.

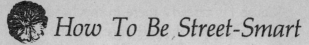 *How To Be Street-Smart*
THE MORNING CLASS,
TRAVELERS AID, Rhode Island

1. Mind your business. You go your way, they'll go theirs.

2. Don't be too friendly.

3. Don't trust anybody because they want to keep you down in the dumps with them.

4. Learn how to hustle getting food, money, shelter.

5. Stay away from the big cities.

6. Learn how to keep away from cops.

7. Beware of someone who is overfriendly to you, someone who tells you you can make easy money fast.

8. Be a leader, not a follower. Go your own way.

9. The *wisest* thing you can do is to stay in school and find a job.

10. Learn how to survive—period.

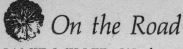 # On the Road

JANIE MILLER, Washington

My husband and I and our best friends, Kathy and J. D., drove to New Orleans on business. We stopped at a cafe in a little town between Dallas and New Orleans.

When we went in, we felt very uncomfortable. There were only white people inside and they were staring at us. No one said anything as we ordered our food; the tension was so thick, you could cut it with a knife. I was scared, but I was also hungry. It reminded me of those movies about how blacks were treated in the South in the old days. But this was today.

Before our food came, the lights went out. That made us even more uncomfortable—sitting in a dark room full of people you think don't like you. They brought candles to every table but ours.

No one said anything. Then J. D. broke the silence by saying, "We must be so dark, they can't see us!" That broke the tension. The room filled with laughter. People began to talk to us. And they brought us two candles.

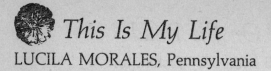

This Is My Life
LUCILA MORALES, Pennsylvania

I am from Puerto Rico. I have nine brothers and sisters. I am the youngest of the girls.

When I was small, I was very happy. I loved to go to school. I loved to climb trees and play. When I became more mature, I went out to eat and go dancing.

When I got married, everything changed. I went to live with my mother-in-law. Then I got the news that I was going to have a baby. That was the best day of my life.

I got sick a lot. When I was six months pregnant, the doctor decided to keep me in the hospital until I gave birth. I will never forget the day my daughter was born.

I was in labor for so many hours. But when I saw my daughter, I was filled with joy. They took me to my room, where my husband was waiting. When it was time for me to take a bath, I fainted. My husband picked me up and laid me on the bed. I was in the hospital for three days.

I went home without my baby. I felt so sad

and cried. My mother-in-law had the baby's room all fixed up. The next day, the baby came home.

My daughter is everything to me. I look at her and see how big she has gotten and I can't believe it. I would like to have another baby, but I have problems getting pregnant.

Two years after I had my daughter, I had a baby boy. He died when he was four months old. I do not like to talk about him because I end up crying.

A year after that, we came to the United States. I got pregnant again but I miscarried in the first month. I haven't gotten pregnant since, but I would like to because I love babies.

I really do not like it here very much. I would like to go back to Puerto Rico to my mother and my friends.

A Week to Remember

DUDLEY AGARD, New York

Everything fell apart last week.

First, the repair guy didn't bring back my TV. Now my niece who is visiting doesn't have one in her room.

Then the pump in my well was shot and I needed to order new parts. While I was checking the pump, I made a big mistake and almost severed my finger. I had to go to the emergency room and have it attached. It seems to be healing well.

While I was trimming the trees in my yard, I disturbed a bees' nest and suffered multiple stings and cuts.

My trailer was damaged when I loaned it to a friend. He overloaded it and bent the frame.

When a lot of people dropped by on Labor Day, I thought I was facing another disaster. But they brought food for a barbecue. I hope this ends the summer without any more problems.

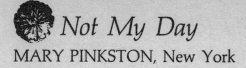 # Not My Day

MARY PINKSTON, New York

I took the subway to school, but there were problems with the trains. I was very late. I thought about going back home, but I was determined to get to school.

After school, I took the subway back home. As I was walking to my apartment, a man grabbed me by the neck from behind. He said, "Give me all your money." I had my purse on the left shoulder and a paper bag in my left hand. That left my right hand free to hold my keys. I stabbed him as hard as I could with my keys and yelled, "Get away from me, you dirty so-and-so."

Just then, a car passed by, and the driver saw what was going on. He stopped and backed up to ask if I was all right. I thank God that there are some good people left.

I thank God for saving my life that night.

 *My Job*

K. V., Kentucky

When I think about my job, I realize how important it was for me to learn to speak and understand English.

I work as a seamstress for a dry cleaner. I have trouble making people understand about sewing. I have to explain what will look good and what won't. When they don't understand a seamstress's work, they don't understand that a seamstress can only do so much. I am glad that, with my English, I can explain my work so that my customers understand about sewing.

I have met a lot of nice people sewing. They have enough confidence in me to keep coming back. Being understood gives me confidence and I feel I can do a better job, even though alterations can be very hard work.

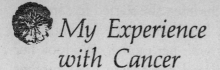

My Experience with Cancer

RANDY K. STEINMETZ, Wisconsin

It all started when my wife complained of a lump on her neck. She went to the doctor, but he could not treat her. He sent her to a clinic, but they did not have the answer. We began to get scared.

The next morning, I called an ambulance. When my wife got to the hospital, she had to wait two hours before she was examined. Afterward, she called me and said they would have to operate right away. If they didn't, she would be paralyzed from the neck down.

The surgery lasted for five hours. It was very hard for me because I didn't know who to turn to. I found out that night that my wife had cancer. I was so scared that I couldn't sleep. I felt like the whole world was caving in on me. I did a lot of praying.

My wife was in the hospital for a month. It was very hard for both of us. And she still continued to complain that her neck hurt.

A few months later, she started to complain that her back hurt. One day, she collapsed while she was with her mother. We took her to the hospital and she had to have another operation. At this point, I said to myself, "Why me, Lord? What did I do to deserve this?" We were all very scared. My wife held the rosary in her hand.

The surgery lasted another five hours. My mother-in-law and I really needed each other and became very close. We prayed together and it seemed like God was right there with us. I wanted to do something to ease my wife's pain. I walked up and down the halls, wishing it were me instead of her.

People were different this time. When my wife had her first operation, friends sent me cards and called every day. When she had her second operation, it seemed like the world was closing in on me. No one called and talked to me. I was very depressed, but I believe that the Lord does not ask you to carry more than you can handle.

When my wife finally came home, she was confined to a wheelchair. Every day, she said she wished she was dead. Finally, she learned to do things in her wheelchair and she felt better. She helped me a lot by keeping the checkbook up to date.

Monday through Friday, I took care of my wife. Some days a nurse came in, and that helped. On the weekends, she went to her parents. The worst days were Sundays when I had all the farm work to do and came in to an empty house. I prayed on those days, and the Lord helped me through them.

When my wife came home on Mondays, she would be so angry. At first, I wondered if she really loved me or not. Then I realized it was the cancer and the pills and that she was facing her own death. One thing that made her especially angry was when she was doing well on the chemotherapy and then would start losing her strength. She would ask, "What is happening to me?" I would try to comfort her as much as I could.

I could never really accept the fact that I was losing her. Our minister tried to comfort us. I was closer to my wife than ever when she was sick.

After my wife died, I felt all alone. At the wake and funeral, there were so many people who had come to give their sympathy. But after that, you are all alone.

I have some thoughts that I want to share with other people who have lost their mates. You have to believe that you are not the only one going through this. One thing that helped me is helping other people who have lost their mates.

My life was drastically changed after my wife died. It took me a long time to accept her death. It helped to cry and get my frustrations out.

When I felt down, I picked up the phone and called someone. I didn't care how much the bill might come to. You should get together with the people you care about and not be afraid to open up to each other.

People give you all kinds of advice, but you have to do what you think is best. Don't be in a hurry to make any decisions you might regret. For example, my sister-in-law told me to get rid of my wife's clothes, and I did it before I was ready.

I had a lot of nightmares and often I was afraid to go back to sleep. There is nothing wrong with taking one of your loved one's special possessions to bed if it helps. One night, I had a dream that my wife was in heaven. She told me that it was the most beautiful place.

It was quite a while before I would go to the cemetery. I would recommend that you take someone with you the first time. After that, it gets easier. Don't be afraid to talk to your spouse. I have a special prayer that I say to my wife.

You can't run away from your grief. You have to face it head-on. Grief goes through stages. If you don't grieve, you will keep finding yourself back at the beginning and it will take longer to heal.

I felt very alone and neglected. It was a long time before I started to go places. Now I try to make myself part of the group, so I will feel more comfortable.

It was two years before I started to feel better. But there were still times when I would ask the Lord, "Why did you do this to me?"

I really wanted to love someone again. When I first started dating, I felt like I was doing something behind my wife's back. But I will always treasure those last few months I had with her very much.

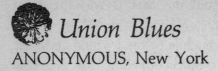# Union Blues
ANONYMOUS, New York

Things are very bad with my job. I got laid off two weeks before Christmas and I don't know when I will be going back to work. It makes me feel bad to stay home.

Every day, I called the union. The secretary kept telling me the delegate was out sick. That made me so mad. I paid my dues every month and they should get me work.

Almost four months later, I talked to the delegate. He told me he would get me something by the end of the week. I waited patiently, but nothing happened.

I have not paid my dues for the last three months. The union wrote and told me that if I didn't pay my dues, they would throw me out. If I don't pay, I will lose my benefits and annuity. This should not happen. When you are not working, you should not have to pay dues. Tomorrow I will go down to the union hall to pay my dues anyway.

What Becomes of the Brokenhearted

ANONYMOUS, New York

I dialed the number and when the phone was answered, I said, "Can I speak to Dee?" The woman responded, "This is Dee."

I said, "This is Yvette. You don't know me. But last night, I was going through my man's pockets and I found your name and number. So, woman-to-woman, it is more than fair to let you know where I am coming from.

"Dee, I don't know how you are going to take this. Either you'll be cool or not. It really doesn't make a difference. The man you are in love with is mine from the top of his head to the bottom of his feet. The bed he sleeps in, the food he eats and the clothes on his back— I make them possible. I pay for all that.

"I am telling you this to let you know how much I love that man. I would do anything to keep him. If you were in my shoes, you would do the same thing. You see how hurt I am. I hope you understand."

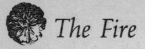 # The Fire

PATRICIA BYNUM, New York

I was sleeping when the fire started. My son woke up my daughter and me. My husband was out driving a cab. When we got outside, I was worried that some of the kids were still inside. But my son had gotten them all out.

The fire happened on July 2. My husband had bought a lot of fireworks, so you can imagine how the fire looked.

We went to our neighbor's house. The next day, we went to a hotel. We were there for four months. The Red Cross provided some clothes for my family.

My husband and I owned that house. My ten children grew up there. All of the things we had earned and received were gone.

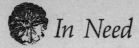 *In Need*

ROSALIND RODRIGUEZ, New York

You needed me,
I needed you.

We met each other at a time when
we needed each other.

We each understood
what the other had been through.

We tried to understand
what life threw at us,
so we could go on living,
trying to understand this world
that is sometimes so cruel to us.

My First Day at Work

CHIA V. XIONG, Wisconsin

On my first day of work, I was excited. I got to the bank at 8 A.M. I went to the personnel office to meet the vice president and his secretary.

The vice president introduced me to everyone in his department. Then he took me to see every department in the bank, including the lunchroom and the mailroom.

The secretary took my fingerprints and explained about the health insurance and other benefits. She told me about my duties in the check-processing department and took me down to meet the supervisor.

The supervisor introduced me to everyone. She explained all the jobs she wanted me to do. Then she started to show me the work while I watched.

At noon, the manager of the department asked me if I wanted to go to lunch with her that day or if I wanted to wait for another day. I hadn't brought a good lunch, so I said I would like to go that day. We went to the

Civic Center and had chicken sandwiches. After lunch, I came back and continued to watch the supervisor.

On my first day, I was scared, worried and embarrassed. All the employees seemed very intelligent to me because I didn't speak English very well. Some of them looked at me like I was too stupid to work there. But others were very friendly and talked to me. That made me feel more comfortable.

Today, I am very comfortable at work. The job is getting easier. I know my speaking is still not good enough, but it is better than before. I don't care what people think of me or say to me. I think to myself that someday, I will speak English as well as they do.

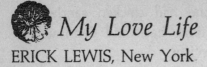# My Love Life

ERICK LEWIS, New York

I am a lover. I am a good lover. Being loved by me is sweet and spicy. The way I approach love is warm and simple. Holding her in my arms makes me feel so happy.

Now that she is so far away from me, sweet thoughts run through my mind. I think about the wonderful times we spent together. Now that she is so far away, there's nothing to do but go down the dusty road with a smile, hoping she will return to me one day.

Then, one day, the phone rings. I wonder who it is. I pick up the phone and joy comes into my heart. It's my sweetheart! What a good feeling to hear her voice again. She says, "I will be coming home very soon to be with my sugar-pop boy." I say, "How soon? I will prepare something hot and spicy to welcome you back home."

My Family

ANONYMOUS, Pennsylvania

My family lives in Poland. I came to the United States in 1984 when I was 42 years old.

My parents still live in a village with my brother and his family. My family is big because my parents had eight children. Now all their children have their own families. They have 26 grandchildren and 10 great-grandchildren.

I came to the USA to help my family financially. I am still helping by sending money and other important things.

I miss my country and my family very much. I miss my family in particular when the holiday season comes. Christmas is the most important holiday for Polish people. It is a peaceful time when we remember the birth of Christ.

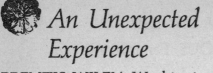 *An Unexpected Experience*

PRENTIS WILEY, Washington

I was in jail once. It was a freak accident.

A man had a store. He had known me since I was a baby. One day, my uncle and I drove to the store to buy stuff for dinner, like soda pop and crackers. We were planning to stay at the store and eat on the porch near the oak tree.

The man said, "You guys eat your dinner, I'll eat mine." He went off to his house. There was thunder and lightning, so I decided to go to my house to sleep and my uncle went to town.

Then some guy knocked on the door. My brother said, "The police are out there." They took me down to jail. They had already picked up three of my buddies. I asked what was wrong, but they wouldn't tell me a thing. One of my buddies said that the store had been robbed. The police took pictures of me.

The police chief knew I didn't commit the

crime. He said, "Everybody knows Wiley. He has a real good name in town. But if I let him go, the others will be stinking about it."

I stayed in jail overnight. I took one look at the mattress in the cell and I didn't want to sleep on it. I slept on the concrete floor all night long. In the morning, the biscuits were hard and the coffee looked like it was six days old.

They let me out around nine in the morning. Nobody robbed that man's store. He misplaced 20 dollars, that's all. He took it home and forgot about it. The next day, he sent for me to apologize.

Marry World

MARY LOUISE GIBSON, New York

When I dreamed about getting married, I never dreamed of a white house or a lot of money. My dream of marriage was three kids, a nice apartment and a good man.

I'm a city girl, born in New York City. I got married when I was 19. My husband was 21, but he was from the backwoods of the South. My husband's world was different from mine. His mother raised him to believe that a wife cleaned house and had a lot of kids. A wife should be covered up so no other man could see anything.

When my husband found out I was pregnant, he made me wear clothes that covered me from my neck to my feet. If a man looked at me, he'd say, "Where do you know him from?" I couldn't go to the store without him. If I went to my mother's house, he would come to take me home as if I didn't know where I lived. If I said, "I'm not your slave," he would show me our marriage papers. He wouldn't fight me because he knew I had too much hell in me.

We went down South to visit his mother. He tried to show off for her, but I wasn't going to kiss his ass just because he was my husband. I packed my bags, got my kids and caught the bus back to New York. I was strong, a very strong black woman.

Each day, things were hell for us both. I knew I was going to walk away from him. I knew I had to wait. I left the day my mother died. I waited until he went to work. I packed and left quickly because I only had eight hours. We were married for only three years.

I knew when I left I was on my own. My mind was on my two children. So I found two jobs. My relatives told me I should have waited. But I knew that I would make it on my own, and I have.

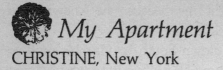 # My Apartment

CHRISTINE, New York

My life changed when my mother moved out and gave me the apartment. Now I'm on my own. I'm responsible now, and I pay the phone bill and other bills. I buy things for the apartment, like food and other things I need.

In the beginning, I had problems. Once, I had a lot of friends over and I had to go to the store. For a minute, I did not know what to buy.

When my mom first moved out, I was scared because I was used to having someone there with me. Now I'm lonely, and I'm so scared at night that I leave the bathroom light on. I will get over my fear of being alone very soon.

 *Isidro*

NANCY SOTO, New York

Isidro was a good friend to me and my family. He came every weekend to sit around and talk.

One weekend, he didn't come around. When he came back, we asked, "What happened to you?" He said, "I spent the weekend at my sister's."

Isidro came less and less to my home. He called and told my aunt he felt sick. My aunt said, "I think you should go to the hospital."

The doctor told Isidro that he needed to stay in the hospital. The doctor and Isidro knew what he had. But Isidro thought that telling us would turn us away. I don't think that way.

It didn't matter what kind of person you were, Isidro, we were always there for you. But when you needed us, you didn't let anyone see you because you were dying of AIDS.

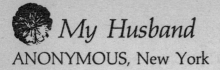 *My Husband*

ANONYMOUS, New York

My husband left me here 20 years ago this month. I don't know nothing about him. When he left, he told his mother I died.

An Unusual Mother's Day

RAMONA B. FUENTES, Washington

Mother's Day started out okay. I got up and fixed breakfast for the family. Then we went over to my mother's house. My brothers and sisters were all there. I told my mother that we were going to make a barbecue dinner for her.

When the food was ready, I started to fix plates for the kids. My sister Rosie came back from running an errand. She asked my other sister, Caroline, if she had sent her son Jose to the store alone. Caroline said, "No. Why?" And Rosie said, "Because I saw a little boy looking in the store window when I drove by, and it looked like Jose."

We all looked around and saw Jose, but I didn't see my son Tony. I asked Rosie, "Did the boy have a blue-and-white shirt on?" When Rosie said yes, I knew it must be my Tony.

We ran out of the house and jumped in the car. When we got to the store, I went in and looked for Tony. I asked the lady in the store if she had seen him. She said, "Yes, but he didn't come in."

I went back to the car. My sister said, "I have something to tell you—don't get too upset. There was a man coming out of the store when Tony was looking in the window." We went back into the store and asked the lady which way Tony had gone. She pointed and said, "Down the hill."

I told my son Frank to go back to his grandmother's house and get his dad. My sister went down the hill to look for Tony.

I called out Tony's name. When I didn't hear him answer or see him come to me, I put my hands together and asked God to help me find him. When my husband came, I asked him if he had seen Tony on the way. He said no.

A man came up the hill, waving his hand at us. He asked if we were the people looking for a little boy in a blue-and-white shirt. We said yes. He told us he had seen him a few blocks away. My sister had stopped everyone on the street and asked if they had seen Tony. He told her where he saw him. My sister was on her way there and had asked the man to come tell us.

My husband ran off in the direction the man showed us. I thanked the man very much.

I met my husband, sister and Tony back at my mother's house. Tony would not let me go.

When you lose a kid, it really scares you. You don't want to think of anything bad happening, but the thought keeps coming in your mind until you find the missing kid.

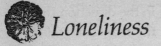 *Loneliness*

BELLA SCHLESINGER, New York

It's a sunny day—a shame to stay indoors. The walls are closing in on me. The place is so empty since . . . No! I don't want to think about it.

Out in the warm sun, out but not free. The memories haunt me. Everything reminds me of . . . no, I just won't think.

The smells, the crowd, the music. Where is that melody coming from? I thought I would never hear it again. It brings back so many memories. I want to forget, I want to remember. . . .

There is the musician. How could he know that melody? I thought it was forgotten with everything else. I want to ask him. I have to ask him. I will go and put some money in his guitar case and then I will ask him about the melody. It is part of my childhood, part of my life, part of my memories. I want so much to remember; I want so much to forget.

"Excuse me . . ."

A Close Call with Death

ANONYMOUS, New York

I remember growing up in Jamaica. My house was near a big pond.

One day, my mother sent me to the shop to buy fish. I saw a lot of kids playing in the pond. I put my things on the ground and went to play in the water.

I didn't know how far I had gone until I started sinking down. Water got in my eyes, my ears, my mouth. I felt like I was choking. I gasped for air. I could not see anything. It was very dark and I was afraid. I tried to tread water.

I had a lot of water in my throat. I felt someone pumping, pumping, pumping on my chest. Then I started to cough. I turned on my side and coughed up the water. I was coming back to myself. It was a good God who saved me from drowning.

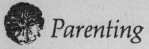 # Parenting

ANGEL ASUNCION VARGAS,
Washington

Parenting. I understand the word in English, but I have trouble translating it into Spanish, my native language. I still can't find the right word to translate "parenting."

I come from a large family where parenting didn't exist, or where it probably existed in a wrong way. So I didn't realize the importance of this word.

I was hoping for something better in my future. I wanted to study, to be somebody. I hadn't been able to study in school because my father wasn't concerned about education. I wanted to try to give myself an education alone.

When my girlfriend told me that she was pregnant, all my plans broke down. I was concerned about the baby and didn't know what to do. It was so difficult—I didn't have my family's support. I became a father when I was 21 and didn't know how to face that big responsibility.

Now I realize the mistake I made by running away. But I am supporting my wife and son financially. It's the best thing I can do after refusing to get married.

My son's birthday is coming next month. Once again, I won't be with him. At least I'll receive one more picture—this time of his third birthday.

My younger brother is 20. He got married last month. I gave him advice from my experience. I told him it would be a good move in their lives if they didn't have children too soon. They are too young for the big responsibility that parenting means.

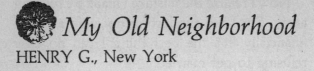# My Old Neighborhood

HENRY G., New York

I went back to my old neighborhood to see how it had changed in the 20 years since we had moved away. The city had destroyed the house where I used to live. They tore down the Wrango Beer Company, which took up five blocks. We used to play baseball in their parking lot almost every day. Now the city is planning to build a shopping mall there.

I felt sad when I saw everything gone. I had to look hard to find the spot where our building used to be.

A lot of old memories came back to me. I wondered how our neighbors were doing now. We were like one big family. Maybe I'll see some of them one of these days. That would make me feel good. We could talk about the old neighborhood. It was a nice neighborhood. There were hardly any drugs or robberies. The building was kept up nicely. There weren't abandoned buildings like you see today.

Where I live today, you can't be friendly with all your neighbors like you could then. Those were the good old days. Lots of things have changed since then.

 *Why?*

KATHY, Rhode Island

One-and-a-half years ago,
I went to visit you
for a holiday.
The next day,
I had to identify your body.
Why?

Becoming a Parent

ANGELA SUTTON, Washington

Excited and scared is how you feel when you get the news that you're pregnant. You think, Am I ready for this?

So many things to buy and prepare, it can be stressful but also fun. There will be hard times as well as things to remember forever.

When you first find out, it is a good time to open a savings account for the baby and keep on saving until the child is old enough to use the money for something important.

This is an emotional time for both parents as they try to prepare for the baby in the right way. The body goes through so many changes, it is sometimes frightening. Feeling the baby kick is really the best part.

I think anyone becoming a parent should be patient and get ready for some changes.

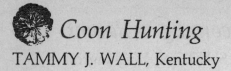 # Coon Hunting

TAMMY J. WALL, Kentucky

Me and my brothers went coon hunting some years back. It was the first time I had ever been coon hunting and the first time I had gone hunting at night. I had hunted in the morning before—for deer, rabbits, doves. I love hunting. Some people say it is not right for a girl to go hunting, but it is one of my hobbies.

My brothers put the dogs in a cage in the back of their truck. I have my own hunting dog named Black Jack. I went in the house to get my gun and a flashlight.

We started hunting about 9:00 P.M. We let the dogs out of the truck. We walked a long way and then we split up into groups. I went with my brother Romeo. That was when the horrible time started.

Romeo's flashlight went dim. We only had mine, and we couldn't see good at all. Black Jack started to bark, so I thought he had treed a coon. I shined my flashlight up the tree. I saw a coon sitting there. Romeo told me to shoot.

As I was getting ready to shoot, the coon jumped into another tree. Romeo hollered, "Shoot the coon, Tammy! Shoot the damn coon!" So I pointed my gun at the coon and shot, but I missed the coon.

Then I heard a sound and said, "No coon sounds like that." Romeo said, "You fool, it's Larry."

We ran to see what was wrong. Larry was sitting on the ground. Romeo asked, "What's wrong, Larry?" Larry said, "You damn fool, I've been shot in the arm." I started to cry.

Larry asked, "Romeo, what's wrong with Tammy?" Romeo said, "Tammy shot you." Larry said some bad things to me. I told him I was very sorry. What else could I say?

Now my brothers won't let me go hunting with them ever again.

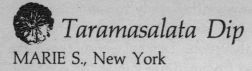 # Taramasalata Dip
MARIE S., New York

If there is a food that I do not like to eat, I do not cook it. My husband loves a traditional Greek dip called *taramasalata*. In all my 31 years of marriage, I had never made it for him. His sister makes it very well. Every time he ate that dip, he made sure I heard about it.

Finally, about six months ago, I asked my sister-in-law to give me the recipe and show me how to make it. She did. I now make taramasalata just as well as she does. My husband is thrilled; so are my guests.

How Old Would I Like To Be?

ANONYMOUS, Rhode Island

I wish that I could be one day old, with a different family. I was brought up by the state. I didn't like it very much at all. I learned way too much in a short period of time at a very young age. I wasn't ready for it and I shouldn't have had to be.

I wish that I could start my whole life over with a close-knit family. I would learn on my own time and not when others think that I should. I would have the stability that a family has and the happiness of having a mother and father to guide me as I grew. I was never guided, just misguided.

I want to be the baby, and later the child, that I never was.

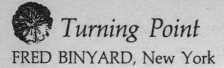 # Turning Point

FRED BINYARD, New York

The turning point in my life was the day I became the single parent of a six-month-old girl named Ebony. Her mother abandoned her because she was addicted to drugs.

I thought, The good times of my life are now ended. I have a child to take care of alone. What am I going to do?

My friends asked what I was going to do with a baby. First things first, I thought. First thing is to feed her. I did not know what I was doing. I gave her milk when she cried and changed her diapers. I knew she needed more.

Being a single parent and working all the time was a real problem. I remembered how my brothers, sisters and I used to play together. So I asked my family to help me with Ebony.

Today, Ebony is five years old. I just take it one day at a time, as my grandmother said.

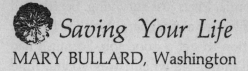

Saving Your Life

MARY BULLARD, Washington

This is a message for those who are feeling depressed and contemplating suicide. It's easy to get depressed. All your brain cells are going in one direction, bills are piling up, relationships are going down and nothing matters. If you feel depressed, please get help. I'm talking from experience; I was a suicidal person.

My parents died when I was 15. My sisters and brothers didn't have enough money to care for me as well as their own families. I moved from house to house.

I got married at age 19. I had three beautiful kids with my ex-husband, but it was a violent relationship. I asked my mother-in-law to help me and take care of the kids so I could move out. I couldn't cope anymore, with him always hitting on me. I didn't know where my next meal was coming from or where I would sleep. I just wanted to get away from the South.

One of my brothers had moved to Washington. I called him and explained my situation. He sent me a plane ticket to Seattle.

In Georgia, I was just surviving. Seattle had a whole different atmosphere. You had to have an education to get a good job. So much had happened in my life when I was young, I did not get an education.

I was jealous of my boyfriend because he had a degree and I didn't. My friends all had degrees and I didn't. My dream was to get an education, but my dreams were shattered. That's when I contemplated suicide and actually attempted it. Never again!

After my suicide attempt, I checked into a home for depressives. While I was there, I saw the light at the end of the tunnel.

My doctor asked me if I would talk with the new interns about depression. I said, "What the heck. I'll do it." When I got to the room, about 50 interns were staring in my face. My heart pounded so hard that I thought I was having a heart attack. But once I got to talking, my mind became at ease.

The interns asked me how I had survived. I just said, "With God's help." Afterwards, I got letters and flowers from the interns, thanking me for talking with them. That was a switch in my life—highly educated people treating me with respect. It was a wonderful feeling and made me realize it wasn't my time to go.

So, if you're thinking about suicide, call someone and get help. There are crisis centers for anyone who needs one. And if you tried suicide once and didn't succeed, then it's not for you. Take what comes when it comes and let it go when it is over.

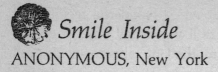# Smile Inside

ANONYMOUS, New York

My mother got very sick when I was about eight years old. I was sent to live with my aunt and uncle. I was misunderstood and beaten for every little thing I did wrong. I hit the streets.

The streets are very hard and cold for a kid, but I was determined to survive. My role models were gangsters, thugs and hoods. They were the only ones who understood me. They taught me how to defend myself.

One of my dreams was to be a boxer. I got a street reputation as a knockout artist. But at age 14 I got stabbed in my left lung, so I couldn't box anymore.

I graduated from boys' homes to jails. I never had an opportunity to do anything positive. Then I was given a chance to come clean. I got sent to a rehab center and changed my life around. Now people look up to me as the nice guy I became. Now I can help people like myself to go down the right road, and it makes me smile inside.

My New Wife

ROBERT P. BURROWS, New York

I was taking a math class at the community college. One Saturday, I locked my keys in the car. One of my classmates asked if I needed a lift home. I said yes. She asked if I would like to meet one of her friends. She gave me Christina's phone number.

I called Christina and we made a date. Two weeks before our date, I had a very bad car accident.

While I was home recovering, I called Christina. We talked on the phone for at least two-and-a-half hours. We did that twice before we went out.

In July we got engaged, and we were married in November. We had our first Thanksgiving, Christmas and New Year's together. We read together and do math together. We love each other very much. Thank God we met.

A Second Language

CHIU-HUI LAN, New York

English is my second language. Naturally, it is difficult for me. I am trying my best to speak in English so I can do what I want.

One of my friends can't speak English. Once she went into a grocery store and bought four cans of food. She ate one can. The next day, she visited some friends in Cincinnati. She took them gifts and the other three cans. The husband looked at her in amazement. They were cans of dog food.

Another time, she went to a diner, but she didn't know how to read the menu. She pointed to the longest name on the menu, thinking it would be a big dish. It turned out to be just toast with catsup.

If I read English well, I won't get into trouble like my friend. It will also help me on the way to success and to become an outstanding person in the United States.

In conclusion, I want to tell you a fable I have heard:

One day, a mother cat and her kittens were taking a walk. A big dog appeared and the kittens were frightened. The dog went "Grr! Grr!" The kittens cried, "Mew! Mew!"

The mother cat looked at the dog and said, "Grr! Grr!" The dog quickly walked away.

The mother cat said to her kittens, "Now you understand the importance of knowing a second language."

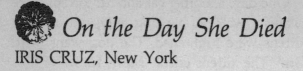# On the Day She Died

IRIS CRUZ, New York

I looked after my sister's children while she was in the hospital. She was very sick. We were afraid that she was going to die.

I was in the kitchen doing the dishes. I went into the other room and looked toward the fire escape. There was a big beautiful butterfly. I knew I had to take a picture of it. I knew my sister had died.

I went to my mother's house. Everyone was there. We all hugged and cried.

The children were my sister's first love. I know that she visited the children disguised as a butterfly. I know she died happy.

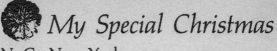 # My Special Christmas

N. G., New York

For the past few years, my family has not gotten along too well. There's been a lot of fighting and bickering. This Christmas, my daughter took it upon herself to bring the family back together.

We called and invited everybody over for Christmas dinner. My daughter went shopping and bought gifts for all the little kids. Everybody brought a dish and gifts. We sat around talking and singing. Then we ate. After dinner, we sat around the tree and opened all the gifts.

The kids were happy to spend time with their cousins, aunts and uncles. I don't know if the family will remain friends, but it sure was nice seeing them all together and enjoying each other. It was the most wonderful Christmas I've ever had. I wish for many, many more like it.

 *Hope*

THOMAS, Rhode Island

Hope—I hope that things keep going the way that they are.

Fear—Fear of the unknown, a fear inside of me that I don't understand.

Anger—Anger is what I have when I have trouble spelling words, words that are in my head that I have trouble putting on paper. I am trying to direct my anger in a positive way.

Love—Love is something I have none of.

War—There is a war inside me all of the time between good and bad.

Peace—Peace is what I hope to have inside some day.

Time—Time is something I have plenty of.

TO OUR READERS

We hope to publish more anthologies like this one. But to do that, we need writing by you, our readers. If you are enrolled in an adult basic-skills program or an ESOL program, we would like to see your writing. If you have a piece of writing you would like us to consider for a future book, please send it to us. It can be on any subject; it can be a true story, a play, fiction or poetry. We can't promise that we will publish your story, but we will give it serious consideration. We will let you know what our decision is.

Please do not send us your original manuscript. Instead, make a copy of it and send that to us, because we can't promise that we will be able to return it to you.

If you send us your writing, we will assume you are willing for us to publish it. If we decide to accept it, we will send a letter requesting your permission. So please be sure to include your name, address and phone number on the copy you send us.

We look forward to seeing your writing.

The Editors
Readers House
Literacy Volunteers of New York City
121 Avenue of the Americas
New York, NY 10013

Four series of good books for all readers:

Writers' Voices—A multicultural, whole-language series of books offering selections from some of America's finest writers, along with background information, maps, glossaries, questions and activities and many more supplementary materials. Our list of authors includes: Amy Tan * Alex Haley * Alice Walker * Rudolfo Anaya * Louise Erdrich * Oscar Hijuelos * Maxine Hong Kingston * Gloria Naylor * Anne Tyler * Tom Wolfe * Mario Puzo * Avery Corman * Judith Krantz * Larry McMurtry * Mary Higgins Clark * Stephen King * Peter Benchley * Ray Bradbury * Sidney Sheldon * Maya Angelou * Jane Goodall * Mark Mathabane * Loretta Lynn * Katherine Jackson * Carol Burnett * Kareem Abdul-Jabbar * Ted Williams * Ahmad Rashad * Abigail Van Buren * Priscilla Presley * Paul Monette * Robert Fulghum * Bill Cosby * Lucille Clifton * Robert Bly * Robert Frost * Nikki Giovanni * Langston Hughes * Joy Harjo * Edna St. Vincent Millay * William Carlos Williams * Terrence McNally * Jules Feiffer * Alfred Uhry * Horton Foote * Marsha Norman * Lynne Alvarez * Lonne Elder III * ntozake shange * Neil Simon * August Wilson * Harvey Fierstein * Beth Henley * David Mamet * Arthur Miller and Spike Lee.

New Writers' Voices—A series of anthologies and individual narratives by talented new writers. Stories, poems and true-life experiences written by adult learners cover such topics as health, home and family, love, work, facing challenges, being in prison and remembering life in native countries. Many *New Writers' Voices* books contain photographs or illustrations.

Reference—A reference library for adult new readers and writers.

OurWorld—A series offering selections from works by well-known science writers, including David Attenborough, Thor Heyerdahl and Carl Sagan. Books include photographs, illustrations, related articles.

Write for our free complete catalog: Readers House/LVNYC, 121 Avenue of the Americas, New York, NY 10013